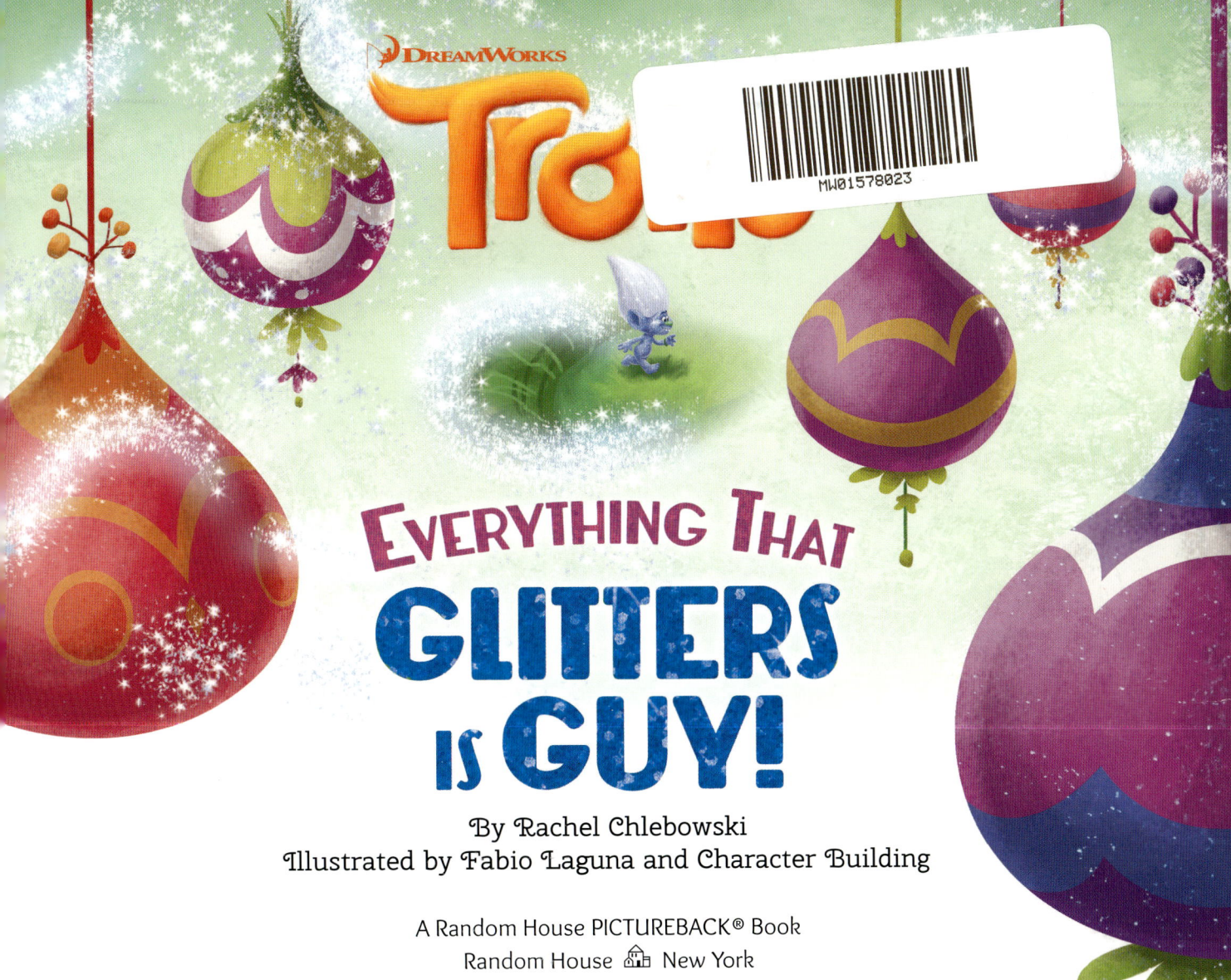

Everything That Glitters is Guy!

By Rachel Chlebowski
Illustrated by Fabio Laguna and Character Building

A Random House PICTUREBACK® Book
Random House 🏠 New York

DreamWorks Trolls © 2017 DreamWorks Animation LLC. All Rights Reserved. Published in the United States by Random House Children's Books, a division of Penguin Random House LLC, 1745 Broadway, New York, NY 10019, and in Canada by Penguin Random House Canada Limited, Toronto. Pictureback, Random House, and the Random House colophon are registered trademarks of Penguin Random House LLC.
randomhousekids.com
ISBN 978-1-5247-1732-2 (trade) — ISBN 978-1-5247-1735-3 (ebook)
MANUFACTURED IN CHINA
10 9 8 7 6 5 4 3 2 1

Glitter effect and production: Red Bird Publishing Ltd., U.K.

Biggie wanted to take a picture of the happy Trolls. On Poppy's count of three, they all said, **"Everything that glitters is Guy!"**

It was a giant **GLITTER PARTY!**

"Welcome to the biggest, brightest, most glittering party ever!" Guy Diamond cheered as his friends joined in with their newly glittering clothing, hair, and accessories. "I'm so happy everyone could make it. And thank you for bringing the glitter!" he added with a wink.

The Trolls decided to join Poppy's search party. At the edge of Troll Village, the glitter trail led deep into the dark forest. The group of Trolls stopped, but Poppy took a deep breath and bravely pushed the leaves aside.

"Oh my gah!" exclaimed Smidge.

Poppy and Branch almost caught up to Guy Diamond at Maddy's hair salon. Everyone there was covered in glitter.

"I guess Guy was just here," Poppy said.

"Yep," said one Troll.

"Sure was," said another.

"I saw him."

"How'd you guess?"

"I look amazing."

Poppy and Branch searched Troll Village high and low. Guy Diamond's trail of glitter was easy to follow, but Guy was hard to find!

. . . and so did a lot of glitter, which landed right on Branch.

"I don't do glitter," Branch sighed, brushing off the sparkly dust.

"Well, come on, then," Poppy said, grabbing him by the arm. "Let's find out what all this glittering is about."

Then Poppy found Branch and Cooper.
"Guy glittered my harmonica," Cooper said. "Check this out!"
Cooper let loose on his harmonica. The brightest notes ever blew from it . . .

But Guy Diamond left as quickly as he had appeared.
DJ Suki was still jamming when Poppy arrived.

"I'm following the glitter to its source!" Poppy said.

"Well, he went thataway!" DJ Suki shouted over the music.

"Glitter!" Guy Diamond sang, popping up out of nowhere. And with a poof, he covered everything in glitter.

"Yes! That's it!" she said. Her new tune sparkled with light.

Meanwhile, DJ Suki was mixing beats and making music with her Wooferbug.

"What is this tune missing?" she asked her Wooferbug.

"I'm going to find out what he's up to!" Poppy said. "Luckily, Guy tends to leave a trail."

She followed his glitter footprints into the garden—but no Guy Diamond.

Next, she searched the cupcakery. Biggie was making fancy treats. Glitter sparkled here and there—but no Guy Diamond.

Poppy was ready to try on a new dress that her fashionista friends, Satin and Chenille, had created for her. As queen of the Trolls, she never knew when she might be called on to go to an awesome party. But when she walked into the dressing room, she saw that the dress was covered in glitter! Lots and lots of glitter.

"There's only one Troll who could have done this," Poppy said.

"Guy Diamond!" Satin and Chenille said at the same time.